A
Road
Trip

RITIKA RANA

 Ritika Rana

—— To all the girls who wish to get out of an undesirable relationship and live the life they desire.

A Road Trip

"A journey from moving on to falling in love again."

Chapter 1

"You were *five* when we first met, and we are standing in front of our college today. I am glad you listened to them." Karan smiled broadly because he was so excited to go to the same college. But I was not happy at all. I had been silent for the last year after my parents' death. It was not easy to forget them and start afresh but still, I was trying not to hurt Karan and his parents.

Whenever I saw Karan's father, my Papa's face came before my eyes. I was so attached to my father. Whenever he came home from work he used to give me gifts. I knew he used to work with Karan's father but something terrible happened and they were no longer partners. He wanted me to become an artist but my dream was something else. I wanted to travel the world solo. My mother never stopped him because she also enjoyed a rich life. She was a little showoff but I love her. After suddenly coming into great wealth, they enjoyed a year of luxurious living before passing away.

My life had stopped suddenly after that horrible incident, but still, Somehow, I passed the 12th standard because it was important for them—to see me as a successful nerd.

It was so difficult for me to become as ordinary as I used to be.

I was not ready to go to college and when I didn't listen to Karan he used to get angry at me. Even in this situation when I was not able to eat anything, I kept listening to his toxic words although Karan had been a huge supporter and caretaker of mine when I was feeling so lonely. Karan was with me since childhood but now it seemed no one left in my life.

My maternal grandparents didn't like my father because my parents left their houses and got married themselves. But I stayed with my grandparents—the only family I had left.

I stayed with them for a few months and when I started to go to college and started to work in a bookstore. After a month I started to live in a separate house as a tenant because my grandparents were getting uncomfortable with me although they loved me and encouraged me to start studying again. So I listened to them and got admitted to the same college where Karan was going to study.

I was a commerce student but I had an interest in fine arts as well because Papa wanted me to become an artist. I couldn't listen to him properly so I chose fine arts in college only for him.

My fine arts classes were after college and Karan did not like arts, drawing, or sketches but he never refused me to do it. Sometimes he imposed his *likes* on me. For instance, he wanted me to stay fashionable and modern. Most of the clothes I had were of Karan's choice. I let him do it and never tried to stop him because I liked him more than friends but sometimes I wanted to stop him.

AFTER ONE YEAR in college Karan and I made many friends. Almost half of our classmates were our friends and most of them were couples. They used to make fun of us, why Karan wasn't dating me, because we looked good together. I used to get serious in this matter but Karan ignored all these things and he laughed *every time.*

He didn't like me the way I did.

He didn't love me the way I did.

He always used to ignore me when it came to becoming a couple, especially in public.

One day I talked to him about this so frankly, *"Why do you always ignore such things? Don't you like me?"* I asked him directly about his feelings.

He replied irritatingly, *"What? We have been together since childhood, It doesn't mean we should need to be in a relationship. Hey, don't say that you are in love with me."* He smiled silly.

I was not.

I only like you. When no one was with me he was there and when my feelings developed in these years I didn't know. I knew he was a little toxic but I was accustomed to him.

I didn't want to stay away from him and I didn't want to break my friendship with him so I shook my head and replied, *"No, I am not in love with you."* I also didn't want to tell him that I *liked* him.

We spent two more years in college together with some sweet and bitter memories (most of them were bitter, ignorant, arrogant, and filled with rudeness) and we entered in third year. It was our final year in college and I wanted to make this year so special and beautiful because after college he was going to his father's company and I had to wander here and there for a job.

My sketches and drawings were selected in a college art gallery last year and hung there with my name in bold letters and with a big photo of mine. I was proud that day because my father came to my mind. The end of last year was perfect for me.

One day I got late for my fine arts class and my feet started to run but I bumped into a guy and we both fell on the floor outside the class. His chocolate brown eyes were glaring at me and his black hair gently danced with the breeze. He was busy collecting my stuff and I was busy admiring his looks. He looked so perfect in an off-white t-shirt and black cotton jacket above it, he was wearing denim jeans. He had a light beard and his height was towering. In a few seconds, I noticed everything in him.

"I am so sorry, are you okay?" He asked with those gentle, soft words I had never heard in years. All I heard were toxic and rude words from Karan's mouth. I wanted Karan to at least talk like that guy.

His hand waved in front of my eyes because I was so lost in him.

My eyes blinked and I stood up. "I am fine, Thanks."

"Are you sure?" He made sure I was not lying.

I nodded and for a few seconds, he stared at my face. "I have seen you somewhere." His eyes squinted but I walked away.

"Hey, wait." He stopped me but I entered the class because I was late.

After a few minutes, he entered and everyone wished him *good noon.* I made a friend in my art class and she told me, "He is Raghav, our teacher's assistant. He is here only for a few days until our exams finish." She also told me that he used to be a student at this college five years ago.

So, he was five years ahead of me.

During the class, he was coming towards me again and again but he was silent, he didn't comment anything.

I was busy making a landscape. It was a view of Emerald Lake, where I used to go for picnics with my parents when I was a kid but we stopped going there when we stepped into a rich lifestyle. I lost interest in that wealthy lifestyle because it stole my simplicity and family time.

When the exam was over I was putting my stuff back in my tote bag and he came to me.

"I hope you pass the exam." He said with a smile. "And I remember where I have seen you—in the art gallery...Aditi, right?"

I nodded with a smile too.

I wanted to spend my time with him but sometimes a thought came into my mind that I was not doing well with Karan. Was I betraying him? But betraying what? friendship?

I never thought about any other guy but Raghav made me think about him and that's why I got the feeling that I was not doing good with Karan.

I started to be inclined toward Raghav sometime later. After college, we both used to go for *chai* outside the chai stall.

We had been seeing each other for the past a

week only and after meeting with Raghav my life seemed to come on a happy and positive track. My life had been miserable before, weighed down by loneliness, but something shifted after a few meetings with Raghav. He brought light into my darkness, and gradually he started making my life better. I started to have a crush on Raghav but not the same as I had on my *toxic Karan.*

I felt a happiness I had not experienced in a long time but then one day Karan did something completely unexpected—He *proposed to me.*

I was so stunned.

My mind raced, confusion swirling inside. A mix of surprise and shock flooded through me. I couldn't ignore my feelings for him because I knew one day Karan would also like me back and the day had finally arrived. I accepted his proposal without thinking twice and since then I never met Raghav.

Chapter 2
Three years later...

My life had been changed *again* with Karan and I was happy with him. Sometimes he behaved a little indifferently for the past few days since I started to visit a psychiatrist. I always hated doctors but I was having bad dreams, I couldn't focus on my work and Karan forced me to see a doctor.

I left my bookstore job long ago and joined a company. Karan and I went to Mumbai three years ago to celebrate my birthday and I wrote a blog about my journey and posted some pictures. After that day a girl named Natasha contacted me because she loved my blog and she offered me a job as a travel blogger in her travel company but I also wrote blogs for others in the office. Natasha and I had become good friends since then.

I was sitting on the plush armchair and my doctor started the session, "So how are you feeling lately?" She asked with a fleeting smile.

"I am so fine. Now I am not having bad dreams

about them." I replied and the corner of my lips lifted.

"Great, now you have to move on okay? So tell me what's the one thing you want back from your past?" Bhumika asked.

My eyes contacted her eyes. Tears were about to roll down my cheeks but somehow I managed to control it and I replied to her, "*My Parents*."

"Look, I am sorry for your loss but as I said you need to *move on* and start focusing on the present. You should start focusing on your work. Natasha told me you haven't done your work these days."

Her words did not bother me because I knew I had to move on and start working on my travels and blogs.

I nodded and she added further, "Okay, now tell me what's the one thing you want from your future?" This time her smile stuck on her face and her eyes expecting an answer *she* wanted to listen to, I guessed.

"Umm...a family. I want Karan's parents to treat me like my own parents. I don't want to be a good daughter-in-law, I want to be a good daughter."

She held my hands with hope and said, "I hope they do."

Her phone rang and she told me that she would continue next week. Bhumika gave me hope all the time because I always needed them. Sometimes I thought I could not live my life alone—somehow I needed people around me.

Most of the time my thoughts revolved around Karan and our simple relationship. I was so habitual of his behavior. I didn't care that much if he didn't talk to me for days or didn't treat me well but when he smiled I forgave all his rudeness.

But still, my heart forced me to ask myself, *Am I happy with him?*

But he was the only one left in my life—he was my everything and if he also left me alone in this huge world then I would be so sure, I was not worthy of love and happiness.

I didn't want to bother my maternal grandparents. They always wanted me to stay with them but I couldn't. I didn't want to bother them.

After coming back home I opened my blog and there was a Pierce in my eyes after reading those awful comments. I understood the loss of my work and I was responsible for it, I had to bear those comments on my previous blog posts. I hadn't gone anywhere for months because of nightmares and sessions with doctors.

I was reading comments when my cell phone grabbed my attention.

Natasha Calling....

Aditi: Hey, Nat.

Natasha: Listen, to me and you can't say No. There is a workshop....happening in Coorg, the workshop is on photography and you have to attend this workshop because it is a great opportunity for you to learn the skill you always wanted and the most exciting part is that.....drum rolls.....I am also going there.

She threw all the information in her one breath.

Aditi: How can I? I am not even coming to the office.

Natasha: It's fine, don't come but please attend this workshop with me. I have never seen Coorg.

I thought for a second because Nat and I had never been anywhere together and she wanted to see Coorg so we should go.

Aditi: Okay I need to ask Karan.

Natasha: What? Are you serious? It's your job and you can't be her puppet, Aditi.

All

the

time.

Her voice was sharp like a knife.

Aditi: Okay, when will we be leaving?

Natasha: Good question, you have one week so do anything but convince him and stop listening to his toxicity every time. I am sending you the link to their website. Fill out the form and let me know.

Aditi: Okay, bye.

I quickly put the cell phone down and started to concentrate on her words and that question arose: *Should I ask him or inform him?* I shook my head and decided to *inform* him not to *ask* him but my phone rang again and it was him.

I received his call with a soft smile on my face and my heart was running like the speed of a Rajdhani train but as he started to open his mouth he faded my smile. I kept on listening to those words but couldn't digest them all at once. Somewhere I knew that this would happen but I always ignored that thought in my mind. When he finished speaking I managed to ask him, "Are you sure about this?" I asked so casually. I didn't want him to know what I was feeling.

He replied in a tone that was not rude at all but it more felt like a guilty and nervous tone, "Yes, I am so sure. That's why I called you. I am sorry."

Natasha's words were like a reminder to me of who I was for him. but for now, I pretended that I didn't care and I just simply told him, "Okay, have a great life, Karan." I put the phone down and cried until I fell asleep.

A week later...

My room had bathed in the soft glow of the moon. This room was as quiet as my life but my life wasn't peaceful and silent like this room.

It had been *six days* since our breakup but still, Karan's voice echoed in my mind and heart—our all promises, laughter, and secrets that had ended now.

He was the one who was there when I needed someone most—he was there to heal my invisible wound when my parents left me alone but today he had become the *wound.*

Every drop of tear was asking me: *when did my love slip through my palm like the fine sand? Why did he leave me too? Did Karan ever love me?*

He never treated me in the way I always wanted from him. I wanted him to stay with me because I didn't want to feel that loneliness ever again.

He had ended this relationship a week ago but still, he wanted to be friends with me. How could I explain to him that whenever I saw him around me I fell for him? Not in that way but I always wanted to forgive him.

EVERY TIME.

Every. single. time.

After an hour I calmed myself and tried to move on from things, finally. I opened the link she sent me six days ago and filled out all the details and at the end of the form a sentence caught my sight: *Thank you for joining us,*

regards from,
Amit and Raghav.

The name *Raghav*—I recalled my memories from the days of college. The art assistant in my fine arts class. A smile appeared on my face because those days were filled with positivity and happiness. I never felt lonely when Raghav was around me. Although I had only spent a week with him, those days were amazing, it did not seem that those days were *three years ago.*

I came back from a delusional world and thought for a second— *Not necessarily, this boy must be the same, Raghav.*

Natasha reminded me of the timings for bus departure through text and my head turned towards the clock. It's 3 AM and the first bus leaves at 9 AM and the second at 9:30 AM.

My lungs pulled a deep breath and I wiped all my tears and decided to start fresh. I decided not to remember him again but I started to see our pictures together in my phone's gallery.

I can't miss this opportunity to learn something new and I can avoid my pain as well. I know it's difficult but I have to get out of this comfort zone.

I walked to the bathroom, splashed some water on my face and just lay down on my bed so I could wake up on time.

Next morning...

I had already packed everything and the piece of toast was in my mouth. My gaze lifted in a hurry and it was 9:15 AM.

Natasha will kill me if I miss the second bus.

I reached the destination where the bus was coming to pick us up and now it was 9:40 AM but there was no evidence of the bus.

A masculine voice echoed in my ear and he came in front of me. "Are you waiting for the bus?"

His facial expression was screaming *You have missed the bus, girl.*

I didn't let him speak further and asked him, "I have missed it, right?"

"Half an hour ago." He nodded. "Where are you going?"

"Coorg."

"Oh, you can book a bus but it takes 8 to 9 hours."

I took my phone out and started to research the website. I was shaking because I had lost my chance and I didn't even know where the exact location was. Natasha was calling me. I picked up her call and she was so enraged at me. I calmed her down and assured her I would come till night.

My fingers were dancing on the keyboard.

As I was standing there and thinking about doing something, I noticed a car was coming toward me and the music was a bit loud. I thought to ask for a lift but the car stopped in front of me and the glass of the window slid down. A man bent his head to gaze at me and he called my name, "Aditi, what are you doing here?"

His deep but still soft voice threw me back to those positive and beautiful memories.

The voice was so familiar but he was unrecognizable. I opened my mouth and asked doubtfully, "Raghav, is that you?"

He nodded with a smile.

His evergreen most attractive smile.

He stepped out of the car and his face glowed and I could easily tell that he was in his thirties.

"How are you? It's been so long." He looked so excited.

"Yeah, I am fine. What about you?"

"I am also good. Are you going somewhere? Should I drop you?" He asked.

Should I?

"Aditi?" He called my name and I came back to my senses.

I told him where I was going and he giggled, "It is my workshop. So hop in the car. It is going to be a long journey."

After seeing him after three years a thought ran through my mind: *Are my happy days back?*

Chapter 3

There was a silence in the car— an awkward silence for the last two minutes and we broke the silence together by saying "So" We glared at each other and laughed.

In just a few minutes I laughed after meeting with him. That's why I could never forget him. However, he had changed a lot only in these three years.

"You first," I said with a giggle.

"So, what are you doing in your life?" He asked.

"I am a travel blogger."

His head turned toward me and he was a little surprised. "I thought you would be doing something in fine arts. You are a talented artist."

That's the one thing I never liked about people—assuming things about others.

I shook my head, "It was my papa's dream but I wanted to travel the world since childhood and I accidentally or by luck I got the job of doing it."

"Well, anything that happens with us is already written in our fate. So nothing is here accidentally or by luck." He corrected me.

"Like our meeting today," I commented

without realizing what I said.

"Exactly." He giggled again.

This was the one thing in him I liked the most—his smiling face. It always stuck to his face. I had never seen him without smiling.

"So, how's Karan now?" He didn't face me this time. The silence filled the car for a few seconds and Raghav awoke my pain which I never wanted to awaken but then I replied with a sigh, "We are not together now."

"Oh." He didn't ask much about him or how and looked out of the window and predicted, "It is going to rain in a few minutes. I think we should stop there."

I nodded and I saw a huge camera on his back seat. So I asked him, "When did you start doing photography because in college you have some different dream."

He also followed my gaze and answered, "Photography.....is my everything. I love to capture animals" There was a smile on his face but this smile was so different from his regular smile. His love and curiosity were visible in how much he adored and respected his work. "And yes I had some different dreams but we have to change ourselves with time. When we don't get something we *like*, it is better to leave it. But *only sometimes, not always.*"

It felt like he was not talking about his dreams.

I agreed with him, "You are right, you need to move on someday. You know I also love photography but I never get the chance and that's why I am joining this workshop today. By the way, why didn't you go with them?"

"So I can help a girl I lost three years ago who missed both of her buses."

I lost? His words stuck in my mind but I ignored them.

"Stop making me guilty."

"Okay..okay, I used to travel by bus but some bad memories happened and changed me. After all, there is a noise of other people inside the bus so it is easy to admire the beauty of nature here in the car alone."

Whatever he was saying I was just agreeing with him and I was so delved into him *again.*

"But I destroyed your loneliness." I looked at him and he chuckled.

"No, even though you completed me. I mean admiring alone or with someone you already knew." He explained.

After talking to him further I was feeling so good. The way I was last night it was all gone from everywhere.

"I still remember how we used to laugh and spend time together after college in that tea stall," Raghav recalled those beautiful memories again and a broad smile appeared on both of our faces.

"Yeah, we used to spend our time in the tea stall more than the classes." I also recalled.

Suddenly the sound of rain falling on the window glass was making me more curious and excited about this journey.

I looked at him and he was already glaring at me and he said so proudly, "I told you. My predictions never went wrong."

"Hmm, so smart of you to predict the monsoon—*the season of rain. Very nice.*"

We laughed and laughed. "You still haven't changed."

"With you, I never want to change."

He cleared his throat and I kept silent.

Why do you always overtalk, Aditi?

The weather, the drizzling rain, this green forest, and this wet black road were everything I wanted when I was with Karan. He also disliked rain so much, and because *he* never liked the rain, he never took me somewhere. I had traveled a lot sometimes with other travel bloggers and even solo but my heart wanted to go with him even for a day but Karan loved his work.

I thought for a second when Raghav was looking out from his side of the window, Maybe *my destiny wanted to give me all this with him.*

Something was there in our destiny because whenever I started to feel alone Raghav entered my life. I didn't have any complaint about this and I am so sure this was not a *betrayal*.

I wanted to say to him, "*Let's dance in the rain.*"

Because the weather and nature attracted me to look outside from the window and after one minute of silence Raghav asked, "So you love rain? Don't you?"

My eyes were stuck on the downpour and I replied, "Rain awakens my inner child and it makes everything so...poetic and...magical." I turned with a childish smile and again Raghav was already glaring at me with his most beautiful smile.

We were a bit close to each other. He didn't look away but I leaned back and cleared my throat.

"Maybe or maybe it's just water falling from the sky but...but I like your version better."

"Don't you like rain? oh sorry, *water falling from the sky?*"

His eyes were on the road but he was smiling and I was not sure how I should control myself to not be attracted to his face and looks.

"Not a fan of *rain* but that doesn't mean I don't love nature."

"How can I trust you?" I raised one eyebrow.

He picked up his camera from the back seat and started to search for something. He was looking for his best and perfect shots to show off his skills because there were almost ten pictures he left behind and still scrolling through the button.

He stopped his finger finally and tilted the camera toward me, "Look, These are my best shots of nature."

I leaned closer to his side and I must say he was so skillful. There were many exquisite photographs of nature and he showed me some of the waterfall photos as well. I leaned more toward his side because water attracted me.

I noticed after a few minutes that we were so close to each other and somewhere I didn't want to end this moment. We looked at each other and just then his phone started ringing. He handed me the camera and said, "You can see the rest of the pictures, I have to take this call."

It was his camera and he gave it to me so that I could see the rest of the pictures. How could he give his precious object to me? It was a bit heavy but I thought, before looking for more photos: I *don't think there are personal photos in this camera.*

I started to press the next button and after some photos, there was a photo of a girl with him and she was wearing a sindoor in her middle partition and a silk saree. She was looking so beautiful.

He hung up his call and asked, "So, do you like my photos?"

I quickly turned off the camera and put it back

on my lap.

"Yeah, they are too good. I have a talented friend."

The rain had stopped after half an hour and he started to drive again. I didn't sleep well last night because of some toxic memories and when I slept I didn't realize.

I woke up with a soft piano instrument and it was already evening and the black—-grayish clouds were looking more fascinating and attractive than before. Raghav was talking to someone on the phone and he was a little concerned.

In those many hours of journey I didn't realize that I had a phone and when I took it out from my cargo pocket—my phone was dead.

WOW, *Amazing*.

My squinted eyes looked at the map and still, half an hour remained until we reached our location and during the whole journey I didn't see those two buses.

"Hey, we are almost about to arrive according to this map but I didn't see those buses. Are we on the right track?" I asked when he hung up the call.

"Oh, you are awake. I was talking to the driver, and their bus got punctured. They will reach by the night." He informed me.

"Can I use your phone...my phone is dead and I have to tell my boss."

"Yes sure, don't hesitate." He handed his phone to me.

I didn't call her in front of him because she spoke too loud and I didn't want him to listen. I texted her everything and told her not to reply and then I deleted the message from his phone.

"Look, we have reached." He turned his car toward a forest-like area and some feet away there was a huge wooden cozy resort in the middle of the forest watching us through the car's window but it was still a minute away from us. He stopped the car.

"This is so beautiful." My eyes widened.

Raghav had already gotten out of the car and he called me, "Come."

The rain had not stopped yet but it was a light downpour and he took out our luggage and we walked through the beautiful forest. Raghav got a notification on his phone and after reading the notification his mind almost burst.

"Is he serious?" He was getting furious but I was standing still with a poker face.

"Hey, relax." I rubbed his shoulder and asked, "What happened?"

The rain started to get heavy suddenly. He held my hand and took me towards the house. We were a bit wet.

After reaching the resort we both were

gasping and glared at each other.

"What happened?" I asked again.

"My brother can't come until tomorrow night, so he *ordered* me to cancel the workshop but we can stay here until he comes."

"What are we going to do now?" I asked him with a little tension because we both were alone in this huge resort.

"Hey, are you comfortable with me staying here alone for a while?"

How can I explain how I feel safe with him—the way he talked, the way he behaved, and the way he was observing my actions?

"Yeah, I am fine with you and after all, we can't do anything."

"Alright." He took the key out from his pocket and we entered the best cozy and warm resort.

Chapter 4

The resort was made of wood and the walls were painted mint green; the resort's interior was camouflaged with the forest. The ceiling was made of glass and the black clouds and voice of downpour hitting on the glass was so fascinating and calming.

On the right side, there was a fireplace along with a comfy off-white couch and a coffee table. But it was more like a house, not a resort.

The spiral staircase went up toward the first floor and underneath the staircase, there was a wooden door and I was having a feeling that there was a small library there.

The backside of that resort had my heart. It has a small pond filled with lotus flowers and leaves. The setup was so intriguing and it felt like I was in a fairytale.

In just five minutes I observed everything around me and I complimented, "This place is so beautiful."

Raghav was not in the hall. He was putting my luggage in our rooms. He was descending the stairs but he listened and replied, "Thank you so much."

So *this is his place*. But I wanted to be sure, so I asked. "Is this place yours?" I was a little surprised.

He nodded. "Your room is already ready so I think you should rest."

"Thanks." I nodded with a smile.

"Well, *friends* don't say these *cursed* words."

"What? Cursed?"

"For me, yes, *thank you* and *welcome. These* are cursed words for me."

And our laugh echoed in the hall.

After a while around seven thirty in the evening, I came downstairs to see what he was doing. He was coming out from the kitchen with two cups in his hands.

"Come, I made tea for us."

"Oh, so you cook too."

"Not every time, but yes sometimes whenever I am in the mood."

"So you are in the mood today." I teased.

We sat on the couch and he put the cups on the table.

"No, I wanted to relive those *chai* memories with you."

I looked him in his eyes and it seemed like he was not joking. It seemed like in these years, *he* missed us a lot.

But he smiled and asked, "Sorry to ask but why are you both not together anymore?"

I didn't want to talk about him but at the same time, I thought I *should* because I did not need to ignore him.

I sighed, "He didn't tell me the reason but he said he's not comfortable anymore with me."

"I never met him but I can say, he lost a gem." He was looking at me but he looked away.

"And what about you? I saw that girl's photo in the camera. Is...is she your wife?

He became silent but he cleared his throat and a tension was on his face stuck like glue. "She *was*."

"Was?" I asked.

"She left me after four months of marriage. She had cancer."

"I am so sorry. It must be hard for you."

"No, not that much. I was forced to marry her by my father. But the way I lost her was a bad experience." He stopped but continued, "We were going to her house by *bus* and she was fine but suddenly she fell on my shoulder and never woke up. She was so good with me. We used to stay like friends but my feelings never developed for her."

I didn't know what else to say. I was a little jealous because he was so lost in her thoughts. I stood up and asked to go to my room. But still, I was feeling bad for her.

"Is everything okay?" He asked.

"No. I am just tired."

I didn't want to hear anything from him about her *but why?* I had no idea.

But then we heard some noises and people started to come. I was waiting for Natasha and after four or five faces I saw her.

She saw us and gave us a playful smile because Raghav and I were standing so close.

I walked to her to help her with the luggage and Raghav got busy attending to other people.

"So, he is the hot guy. Your one-week friend from college." She teased me.

Our bond was so special. We were best friends, sisters first and then boss and employee.

I nodded and she came inside. I took her to my room and she settled in. She asked everything about my journey and we talked until she was freshened up.

I wanted to tell her the secret but I was a little hesitant. After thinking for a few seconds I opened my mouth, "I wanted to tell you something."

She got excited to listen.

"I...I had a crush on Raghav."

She tilted her head and raised her eyebrow. "You know what? I knew this. The way you had told me about this guy I knew you had feelings for that *hot* guy."

"But I never said that to him." My gaze looked down.

"Why?"

"Because I liked Karan too and we had been together since a very small age and then he proposed to me. I was super happy that finally, he saw me as his future."

"Yeah, *future.* I am seeing it now." She said in her sarcastic tone because she didn't like Karan. "But destiny wants to give both of you a chance to get back together and I am so sure about it." She said,

"What? Are you crazy? He's five years ahead of me and I said I had a *crush* on him."

"But you have to believe me. N*ow* this is not a crush anymore. You must start to spend more time with him."
"But what if I get attached to him? And what after this?" I sighed and took a sip of water. "You know I can't lose anyone *now* especially, Raghav."

Natasha was a little angry at me but she explained the whole scene of my story through her POV, "When you were with Karan you were scared and stressed every time but today you have a different glow and happiness on your face and *you* told me if Raghav was treating you *that* good then at least respect his efforts and try to be good friends with him if you want to stay out for Karan's life."

The way Natasha explained to me and gave me comfort—I thought she was right. I had to do something to move on from him and stay out of his life forever.

AFTER DINNER I sat on the edge of the pond.

The forest area and cold breeze were calming me, and the fresh smell of wet grass and earth filled my heart with happiness but from inside I was not happy.

I could sense someone was behind me and walking towards me. I immediately turned my head and Raghav was there.

"Are you not feeling cold here?" Raghav asked and before I could say anything He offered me his jacket. "You look worried. What happened?" He sat beside me.

"Nothing, just trying to come out from the breakup thing. I have never experienced it before." I smiled silly.

"Don't force yourself because you both are not together now. The more you *try* to forget him the more you need to fight with your feelings. So just go with the flow. If he stands right here in front of you then try to just be normal don't force yourself to ignore him. Everything will be better and....don't thank me later." He giggled and made me giggle too.

My eyes go deeper in his eyes.

"Well, It is so dark and cold here so we need to go back inside." He offered his hand because the tiles on the floor were also wet and slippery. I took his hand and we walked through the door.

I didn't know what was happening to me. It had only been a few hours and I just wanted to listen to him. He never forced me to do anything even though he let me do it.

I wanted to follow his orders.

I wanted to be around him.

What is happening to me?

Chapter 5

NEXT MORNING we got up and the weather was normal but not clear. Nat and I got ready and came downstairs. The workshop had not been canceled but delayed and it would start from the next day. His brother informed Raghav about the workshop.

We didn't have anything to do for the whole day but after breakfast when I was roaming outside the resort I noticed Raghav was sitting on the chair beside the pond and reading a book. I was a non-reader but the cover of the book was so fascinating. I didn't want to disturb him but I couldn't resist getting closer to the book.

"Aditi." My name from his mouth gave me a sensation and nervousness.

"You read books—interesting," I commented.

"Yeah, Not that much but yes I read." He closed his book. "Do you read novels?"

I shook my head with guilt. I sat next to him and asked, "How did you start reading novels?"

He was about to tell me but then he stood up and a guy older than Raghav came towards us. "You?" He had mixed expressions on his face. "You said you…"

"Do you want me to go back then?" He asked playfully. The guy glared at me and extended his hand towards me, "Hi, I am Amit."

So he was his elder brother.

We shook hands and he told us that he was here with one of his close friends and he wanted to meet Raghav so we came as early as possible.

"You guys talk. I will meet you later." I walked through the door.

"Here he is," Amit said.

I turned and my mind was completely blown when I saw him coming with a huge smile on his face and as he glared at me his smile faded away. I was shivering and my heartbeat was so fast. I ran inside the house and closed myself in the room.

"What's wrong with you? You scared me." Natasha stood from the bed.

"How….how…" My cracked voice stuck inside my throat. I could not control myself. I was breathing heavily and gasping for air and Natasha was getting worried. She gave me a water bottle from the mini fridge and I drank it slowly.

"Now tell me what happened?" She asked again.

"Ka…Karan is here." I finally said.

"What? What is he doing here?" She was in shock too.

"He's Raghav's brother's close friend."

"Okay, but why is he here? Listen." She cupped my face. "Don't let him know that his presence is affecting you."

"But..."

"No, no if and but just listen to me. Do what I say or let him win. You need to be strong now. You are no longer in his cage—you are free now. I can understand you have been together since childhood but look at yourself—what his presence made you. Look at yourself, You are shivering."

I nodded but I liked him even if he didn't.

"I can understand you like him but were you *happy* with him?"

I shook my head. "I want to stay happy." I almost cried and my voice cracked again.

Nat sighed. "Then please stay away from him and....start spending your time more with the person who makes you feel elated. Raghav is a nice guy and you know it, even I know it. Not everyone has the strength to maintain a years-old relationship for eternity." She explained to me a lot.

I calmed myself no, *she* calmed myself and explained everything to me like my elder sister and now I was clear on what to do.

I didn't get out of my room until dinner time because somewhere I needed some time and space. Everyone was already on the dining table before the food got on the table except Raghav. He came with a bowl of curry and he started to serve everyone one by one. He looked at me and gave me a calming smile. Nat and I came downstairs and I was trying so hard not to look at Karan.

When all the food was on the table the guy who cooked for us sat next to Karan and there was no chair left for Raghav because an unnecessary person came between us all.

Nat and I took our plates and sat on the couch and Raghav followed us. Everyone was staring at us but we ignored them all.

Around him, I never felt sad or low. I was glad he followed us.

When Natasha went to fetch the glass of water Raghav asked me, "Why did you leave like that?"

"Nothing I was going by the way."

In our college time, they both never met each other because my classes were after college and Karan never showed his interest to pick me up after college so they both never got a chance to meet but destiny was messing with me now.

After dinner, one of the girls from the other company's group suggested playing *truth and dare* I didn't like this game because no one had ever been so honest but Natasha took me to the corner and whispered in my ear, "This is the best chance to make Karan jealous just sit so close to Raghav."

I laughed at her silly words because I had

never done this to him and it was seriously silly. "But I am not playing because he loves this game and he will play."

"Karan and I are tired so you guys play," Amit told them.

We both looked at each other and immediately sat near the fireplace on the floor where everyone was sitting. Raghav was in the kitchen helping in washing the dishes and as my attention switched to the kitchen he came outside from the door—his shirt sleeves were folded to the elbow, and the veins were getting intense to come out from his skin.

He is looking so perfect and hot in his dark blue shirt.

Again I was in my delusional world and I got distracted when from nowhere Karan grabbed the seat next to me. Raghav saw us and Nat left a gap for Raghav so he could sit next to me. So basically I was stuck between two boys.

I stared at Natasha and she was showing me a thumbs-up gesture. It was a terrible moment. Karan leaned and whispered in my ears, "What are you doing here?"

"I can ask the same question."

Raghav noticed us and he sat so close to me. Karan saw this and he was staring at Raghav. He leaned again to say something in my ear, "What's happening between you two?"

I whispered back, "Why should I tell you? Did I ask you about the girl who has been clinging to you all the time at the dinner table and you are not even stopping her?"

His red eyes and boiling blood didn't affect me now. He stood up and walked upstairs. The game had already started and everyone was enjoying it so much and the bottle spun and stopped towards me.

A boy asked, "Truth or dare."

I was good at telling the truth so I chose the truth.

"Truth."

He asked, "Do you have anyone special in your life you love?"

I didn't need to think twice to answer this simple question because he was sitting next to me. I wanted Raghav to get the hint so I glared at him and answered, "Yes, I have someone in my life."

Raghav's smile got bigger.

The bottle spun once again and it stopped pointing at Raghav, the girl who was spinning the bottle asked him, "Truth or dare?"

"Always truth." He smirked.

"So, Do you have anyone in your life you like the most?"

This game should be named *Love Talks and Dare* because everyone asks only love-related questions.

This question made Raghav and me a little uncomfortable not with the question but he was getting uncomfortable looking at me.

"No, no one."

I stood up. "You guys play, I need to use the restroom." I felt upset because of the answer.

I didn't go to the restroom because it was just an excuse but why did I make the excuse? I didn't know. I just wanted to come out for a moment.

It took me years to feel for Karan but it was the same feeling I was having right now for Raghav *in just a couple of hours.*

What is happening to me? He just confessed that no one in his life he likes so why am I feeling hurt?

I had a feeling that he betrayed me. I was falling for Raghav. In college days he was my crush and we both had spent a week together but some time later he was married to someone else. He told me it was a marriage of force....

It is just a feeling to avoid loneliness. I think That's why I want someone else in my life to fill the space but what if Raghav truly feels for me?

I shook my head and threw all the thoughts related to him from my mind. I needed to stay calm because he was in my present time.

I didn't want to just disappear like that so I

came back to them, "I am not feeling well so I am going to my room. Sorry, everyone."

Natasha also came with me. Everyone was fine with this but Raghav was not. I could feel that he also had something to say to me and he was just finding time to talk to me.

"I think we all should go and have some rest now. The workshop is going to start tomorrow." He looked at his wristwatch. "Oh god, it's midnight, sorry guys I am off."

AFTER MIDNIGHT when I was standing in the kitchen to get the normal water I heard someone was coming downstairs.

The creaking voice of the wooden floor was getting so close to me and there was a fork on the kitchen top. I picked it up in my hand and when I felt someone was close to me I turned immediately. The air was choking me and I was feeling so stupid because I almost attacked Raghav with a fork but he stopped me at the right time by holding my wrist.

"Oh god, it's you." I was gasping a little and he put my hands down.

"Nice." He mocked me. He filled his bottle from the tap and turned toward me.

"Are you fine? You said you were not feeling good."

"I am fine now."

"Can I ask you something?" He asked. He sipped water and came close to me. "Is he the Karan of your life?"

I got uncomfortable again and my hand started to tremble.

"I...I think I should go and sleep." My voice cracked and trembled. My cheeks were turning red because I was feeling so strange and uncomfortable right now. My head was hanging low and I was not able to contact his eyes.

My feet started to walk through the door but Raghav held my arm—a soft grip that I could easily lose my hand but I didn't want to. My feet froze there and my eyes were still staring at the floor.

He came in front of my body and the grip of his hand was loose now. I was free to run but I didn't because I didn't want to run. I wanted to see him in his eyes because my heart was telling me to hold on—to stay there with him.

"Answer me." He asked so softly as if he had some hopes for me.

I took a deep breath and ignored what my heart was telling me. Today—right away I wanted to listen to my brain. "Yes."

He stepped away a bit after heating the atmosphere around me and said, "I noticed the way he was talking to you and honestly I didn't like it. I am no one to judge but how can you fall for such a guy who doesn't know how to treat a girl, especially your girlfriend? I would have never treated you like that if you would have been *my girl.*"

I smiled shyly and came out of the kitchen.

I came into my room and the smile was not going anywhere when he said *my girl.*

Chapter 6
Next day....

In the morning after breakfast, we all got to know that the workshop had been delayed intentionally because one of the brothers wanted to see our patience level. For a wildlife photographer patience should be their priority so they can have the perfect shot, they have to wait for hours and Amit wanted to teach us the importance of time and patience.

We were all gathered outside the resort and everyone was given a small camera. Amit and Raghav were standing on the porch and all of us—ten strangers were standing in front of them.

"So today is our first day of the workshop and I want to give you *your* time to be friends with an unknown object which is in your hands. So all you have to do is go in pairs and click some photographs you think are the best. That's it."

It was such an easy task to do on the first day and I was becoming so excited to experience this feeling. A huge smile appeared on my face, and my heart was jumping up and down. Natasha was here only to roam the Coorg.

"So come here girls and pick your chits from the jar. Your partner's name is on the chits."

I walked toward the jar hoping that Karan would not be my partner. I picked the chit and came back to the place where I was standing.

"So on my count to 3, everyone will open their chits and show me. 1...2...and 3."

Everyone opened their chits and as I opened mine I immediately flipped the chit toward Amit.

"This girl is so lucky." Amit pointed his finger at me and I flipped the chit at me and I was on cloud nine after reading the name. My partner was Raghav who was so talented in his work.

I always wanted to learn this seriously and if a talented person will guide me then yes I am lucky. I was so elated. On the other side, I looked at Karan who was watching me—no he was staring at me and his face was turning red because I was happy without *him.*

"So we are going to Nagarhole National Park where you will find animals and you can have fun and experience safari there. So get on the bus and be ready for the adventure." Amit informed us and everyone cheered up but Karan was so irritated and the girl who was clinging to him was around him like a bee. I ignored them and searched for Raghav. I quickly remembered that he was uncomfortable on the bus. I sat with Natasha but a few seconds later he got inside the bus and sat behind us.

The sun still hadn't come yet and we all had left for the safari. I traveled a lot but I had never experienced safari before. I was super happy with my decision to come here.

In an hour of journey, we all sang songs and enjoyed ourselves and Raghav captured our beautiful pictures with his camera.

AFTER AN HOUR we almost entered the forest and this feeling of true nature and calmness around the forest was so soothing. We had done the formality at the entrance and Raghav, and I hopped on the jeep. Karan tried so hard to come with us but Raghav asked Amit to take Karan with him and I was surprised because I didn't get this: *Is he doing this for me or he doesn't want to be around him because he is jealous of him?*

But I was so relaxed that Karan was not with us in this jeep.

As the jeep started my heart was clapping inside my rib cage. I was getting so excited for this ride.

"You are looking so happy." He said.

"I am," I replied.

"With me?" He asked with a teasing smile.

"My friend."

The first bump made me nervous because I accidentally rested my hand on Raghav's thigh. The path was a little bumpy at first but after a few seconds, the path turned plain there. I removed my hand from his thigh and a shy smile appeared on both of our faces.

Natasha was in the other jeep but behind us and she couldn't watch us. The Jeep was open so we could stand and click the pictures.

The calmness of this forest had turned into a melodic harmony of birds and animal's voices. There was a roaring tiger from the left and crickets were everywhere. You could sleep here with these sounds. The sun came fifteen minutes ago and it was unbearable.

Thanks to Raghav because he suggested wearing a hat and avoiding bright colors. He also suggested I should wear clothes like green or brown so I could camouflage with the background and couldn't look alien to animals.

Raghav looked into my eyes and asked, "Are you enjoying this?"

"I am enjoying it so much because I am with you. *Oh god.* "I...I mean yes I am enjoying it."

"I am glad you are enjoying it." He stopped. "With me." He smirked and winked.

We both smiled and shared eye contact but the driver distracted us, "Guys look, the tigress is coming with her cubs, be ready with your camera."

Now we could enjoy the real Safari.

He lifted his camera and stood so heroically holding my hand in his other hand and he put the camera in front of me—he was hugging me from behind but he was so focused on his work and guiding me to click some perfect shots.

"Be patient and stable and when you feel *this* is the right time to click just click the button. Are you ready?" His lips and his soft voice were so close to my ears and that could be the reason I lost all my focus right away. But I controlled myself and as he said *click* I clicked three to four shots immediately.

For the first time, I saw a tigress with her cubs so closely. They all were playing, rolling their small cute bodies on the ground and one of them was yawning, and then here came the male of their family. I witnessed a sweet family.

"They are so cute together," I commented.

My head turned toward the left to see him and Raghav was already looking at me and he agreed, "Yes, they are perfect with each other."

After a while the jeep stopped and we waited to capture some peacocks because they were so close to us. The sun was so harsh on my face because of the open jeep.

My hand itself started to fan me because I couldn't tolerate the scorching heat. Raghav stood up with his heavy camera, he blocked the sun and covered my face with the heat.

Is he doing all this for me? Thoughts came into my mind and as he was doing these small gestures I could not control myself. How could I stop myself from getting attached to him?

I had done this same thing for him in my past days in college. When a student came to talk to him about some college stuff the sun was disturbing him so I blocked the sun for him but he didn't even look at me that time.

He was the one who I had a crush on for the first time in my life. This was the secret I wanted to scream right in front of his face but a secret should be kept hidden otherwise it was not a secret.

In the half journey of the safari, we were waiting for one elephant and the guide had already warned us that he's a little aggressive so stay calm all the time and stick to your seats.

Natasha loved elephants and he came out behind a tree and it was far away from us but she waved her hands at the elephant and made a noise—like the elephant was waiting there for her only.

"Nat, stay calm please," I warned her.

"Sorry." She showed her teeth.

After waiting for almost ten minutes the driver suggested we move further and we have to agree with him.

The driver started the jeep and from nowhere, the elephant started running towards us from behind. We both were standing and because of the bumps on the path we experienced a jolt. We fell on our seats and my ankle twisted a bit but I ignored it because the elephant was the main problem here.

Immediately Raghav wrapped his arm around my waist and covered my head with his second arm—he protected my head from a jerk but his neck jerked slightly.

My head was clung to his chest and I had never felt this protection before, never. I never got too close to a guy, not even with Karan.

As I was clung to him my heart was saying something to me:

If this means something in between us then I am seriously not ready to be broken again.

If this means something truly then I am not ready to lose Raghav.

When I opened my eyes after a few seconds. I felt a vibration in my ear.

"You are safe now. The elephant is gone." His soft words whispered into my ears and I released myself from the safest cage ever.

"Thank you. Is your neck fine?" I asked.

"So, you noticed." He chuckled.

"I notice everything."

"Well, it is not worse than your ankle."

What? He didn't see that moment. How did he know?

"I also notice everything." He smirked. "Is it fine?" He assured me.

"I am okay."

I was not feeling any pain then.

The safari was also finished now and as I stood up on my feet to get down the jeep my body fell on the seat and I screamed softly, "Oh god my ankle. It's hurting."

Raghav immediately took out a spray and instantly applied it to my ankle. The purple bruise popped up.

"Oh god, Aditi you have a sprain," Natasha ran towards me and told me because I was only admiring and observing Raghav's care towards me. The way he was caring for me was something else.

He got down and offered me his hand, "Come hop on my back slowly. You can't walk so let me take you to the bus."

"It's ok, I can walk or limp." I giggled to avoid this but he was serious and he was not smiling at all for the first time.

Other jeeps also started to come out and Karan was watching everything as he was getting off of the jeep.

Karan saw me in the pain and he came towards me but he stopped because Raghav forcibly lifted me in his arms and I also let him do what he was doing.

Chapter 7

I was not fine because of my ankle but on the bus, Raghav gave me a foot massage and Karan was watching everything. I never wanted to make him feel like that but at the same time, I was not feeling bad for him.

For. the. First, time.

I was feeling better and could walk now. We got off the bus and still, Raghav was holding me by my waist.

His soft voice came into my ear once again, "Are you feeling better now?"

"I am fine now, Thanks to you." I showed my gratitude with so much love.

"I know you are fine but still you need rest. Just go to sleep after dinner okay." He was assuring if I was fine or not and he was so good at taking care of people.

"Sure and thanks once again."

AFTER DINNER, Raghav came to the living room with a glass of water and a painkiller. No one was here but us.

He sat on the couch next to me and before him, I tore the packet of medicine and handed him a pill.

"I am fine." He said.

"You were stretching your neck the whole time while eating. So take it." I insisted.

"Okay fine but this is so bitter." He made a face that he had already taken the medicine.

"Sweetness never cures anything."

"Ouch." He acted dramatically. "Your deep words." He giggled.

"Well, thanks but now take it and swallow quickly."

He put the small medicine on almost the end of his tongue so that he couldn't taste it, but he didn't know.—this tongue is a tongue, and its work is to taste everything wherever you put it.

His whole body wobbled like a jelly and he handed me over the medicine. "Your turn."

I put the medicine on my tongue and swallowed it in a second, and Raghav made a surprised face. "Wow."

Sometimes he behaved like a small kid who saw something very new in his life and this behavior of his attracted me so much toward him.

We both giggled.

"So now you should take a rest. Good night."

"You too, Mr. Photographer." I smiled. He helped me stand up and cross the stairs.

We reached the first floor and my room was in front of his room. On the last step, I almost fell on his arm. Our lips were only an inch away and both of his hands gripped me so tight.

We both came closer but his words came to my mind that he didn't have anyone he liked so I stepped back. He pushed some strands of hair behind my ear and said, "Oh actually, I…I forgot to tell you that tomorrow we are going to the purple hill." He shared it with excitement.

"I have never heard about it," I said softly.

"You will like the place." He assured me.

"You don't know me.' I giggled.

"Or maybe I do." He laughed and winked to avoid the awkwardness because we were almost going to kiss each other.

I nodded and entered my room where Natasha was already there and standing with one hand on her waist and one eyebrow raised.

Raghav had gone and I closed the door.

"What is cooking between you two?"

I pretended right in front of her face that she was thinking too much and she was in her fantasy. "What? Nothing."

"You think I am dumb?"

"No, as I said, you are just thinking too much. We are good friends." I smiled and lay down on the bed slowly with her help.

She held my hand and slowly made me sit on

the edge of the bed. "Listen, if you like him then go and tell him."

My eyes met the soft rug under my feet. After a few seconds, I said, "I do like him but I am scared if I am worthy of love or happiness. I am scared to lose him."

"Hey, don't think like that okay? Your destiny is not always going to work like that. Trust your gut and listen to what your heart is saying." She explained beautifully.

Natasha was almost four years older than me and she was a married woman. She was so happy with her husband and the way they were managing everything together was so perfect. Natasha was not only my boss but more like a family as I said before—I always look for an elder sister in her—the way she gave me advice and helped me out in every difficult situation.

She had more experience than me and that's why I always listened to her.

"Okay, I think you are right but I must wait for the right and perfect time."

She tilted her head toward me a little and said, "Sometimes there is no perfect time. You have to make your time perfect and tomorrow we are going to a very beautiful place so you have a chance to confess your feelings to him." The corner of her lips lifted and so did mine.

Many thoughts came to my mind, some of

them were positive and some of them were negative.

"What if it is just the care? What if he doesn't like me?" I was not confident and sure.

"*You* are thinking too much now and haven't you seen the way *he looks at you*? He is definitely in love with you darling. Relax and sleep well. You need rest."

I thought and recalled all of the memories I spent with him and yes Nat was right.

"Okay, good night."

As I lay down on the soft bed I didn't sleep because of my excitement and nervousness. My nervousness was increasing so badly but like she said: *You have to make your time perfect* so I better sleep because tomorrow my life is going to change.

I hope it changes.

Sleep well, Aditi.

The next morning I was half awake and my ears worked so well even in sleep. The loud sound of a heavy downpour falling on the window was coming to my ears. My nose started to sniff the fresh and freezing air coming inside the room from the open window.

The loud sound of a thud coming towards my room. Goosebumps popped up all over my skin.

I sat startled on my bed covering half of my face with the bedsheet. But she came in front of me. Natasha was here and her breath was not ready to be controlled by her. Her nonstop breaths were bothering both of us.

"What's wrong with you?" I asked, rubbing my eyes.

"I have one bad and one good news. Which one do you want to hear first?" Her breath was also better and she was not gasping for air now. Her lips turned into an upper curve.

"Go on with the bad one first." I always wanted to save the best for the last.

"Our workshop is canceled because both brothers have to go to meet their father in Bangalore and after an hour we are going back to Ooty."

"And what's good news?" I wanted to hear good news quickly if Raghav and I were going to separate in just an hour.

"I was going to talk to Amit in his room but he was busy with his brother. So I stood at the door and...I...*eavesdropped* because they were talking about *you.*"

"Me? And...?" I was a little surprised because of what he had to say to his brother about me.

"Amit wanted to know from him if Raghav likes you so he asked and Raghav immediately said yes." Her teeth were showing through a broad smile with excitement. As if they were talking about her.

"What? Are you so sure?" My eyes widened, I

jumped out of bed and my body started to jump onto the rug. I was on cloud nine but someone knocked on the door and my attention diverted there.

"So your ankle is fine now," Karan commented.

I controlled my emotions and let him come inside.

"Excuse me." Natasha slowly slipped out of the door.

"What are you doing here?" I wanted to punch him in the face because I couldn't tolerate him now. I didn't want to talk to him nicely.

"I am here to see you if you are okay or not but you are good."

"Why do you care?" My tone changed.

He held my hands and a discomfort was on his face. "Why are you behaving like this to me? I have just finished the *love* relationship, not our *friendship*. Why can't you stay with me like we used to behave in college *before* our relationship?"

I released my hand from him.

"Love? If there was love then it would not have ended and if something is over *now* then it is over, Karan. Yes, we *used to be* best friends but some days ago *you* finished everything even after knowing that *you* were the only one left in my life. I liked you, Karan but now EVERYTHING IS FINISHED."

My eyes were wet and my voice cracked but I

didn't want to look weak in front of him. My eyes didn't let the tears fall on my cheeks.

In those days I learned to be strong even in front of my weaknesses.

"I am sorry I know I have done so wrong with you but I can't tell the reason but trust me we can start fresh. I will punish myself but I don't want to lose you. You have been with me for ages. We have always supported each other, helped each other." There was a guilt in his eyes. He had done something wrong he knew but still, he didn't want to let go of me. I didn't know what he had done and I didn't want to know.

For a moment, it all seemed so correct. I didn't have any feelings in my heart for him anymore and we had been friends since I lost my parents. There's no harm in remaining *only* friends with him. Somewhere I wanted to forgive him because he was guilty of what he had done with me.

"Okay, let's give ourselves a fresh start," I said with a sigh and immediately I noticed at my door that someone was listening to us.

My head turned to the door and Raghav was there.

"Raghav." A smile appeared on my face.

He came inside and asked with his soft smile, "Did I disturb you both?"

"No, not at all," I replied.

"I came to see if you are better."

"She is fine now, see," Karan replied to him in a slightly rude tone which was not needed. I got offended a little bit but I nodded with a fleeting smile and asked "And your neck?"

"It is not bothering me now. Medicine helped." He scratched his eyebrow. "Well, I am glad you both are together again." Now he was smiling fake.

Karan glared at me with a soft smile on his face and said, "Yeah, we can't live without each other."

I stared at Karan because he was talking in the wrong way. I was about to say but Raghav said, "Okay, so the breakfast is ready and we have to leave soon. The weather is also horrible today." His face faded and pale. He was not smiling anymore.

We were having our breakfast and Raghav was not looking at me the whole time. He was so calm and it didn't suit his personality.

After breakfast, we all were ready to go back home. I wanted to go back the way I came here—I wanted to go with Raghav but he was nowhere when I came back from the room.

I saw Amit was checking his bags near the bus. I went to him and asked about Raghav. "Hey."

"Aditi hey, Is your leg fine now?"

Both the brothers were too caring.

I nodded. "Yes, Raghav cured it. Um...Do you know where he is?"

"Raghav? Don't you know? He's already left for Ooty. Didn't he tell you? He was not feeling good so he left."

My heart stopped but I didn't want him to know anything about us although he knew some of it.

"He told me, I must have forgotten." A fake smile appeared on my face too.

"Okay now hop inside the bus. We are leaving…" He looked at his watch. "Five minutes."

Amit was leaving but I didn't want to miss the chance to contact Raghav. "Amit." I gave him Natasha's office visiting card. "Contact me when it's needed."

He grabbed the card from my hand in confusion and put it in his shirt pocket but then he immediately smiled like he understood the mission.

"Sure. I will give it to him once we get back from Banglore."

"Thank you." I nodded.

My soul wanted to cry and scream as loud as possible. My heart and soul were so disturbed but I didn't want to show my feelings and emotions to anyone, not even to Natasha because she was right about the *right* and *perfect* time.

I took out my phone from the backpack and headphones because I didn't want to listen to the noise and played the song..

Chapter 8

It had been 2 weeks since I returned from the trip and I hadn't gone anywhere. I was just waiting for Ragahv to contact me. Although I went to the office sometimes because I didn't want to feel what I was feeling two weeks ago. *Loneliness and sadness, all. The. Time.*

I was in doubt if Amit had given him the contact or not. He was a good guy like his brother but still, I was not feeling good. It felt like something happened with Raghav.

I shook my head and ignored all the pessimistic thoughts.

Natasha observed me for many days and many times she told me to stay happy but my mind wasn't ready until I confessed my feelings to Raghav that I love him.

Natasha hadn't come to the office yet and her phone was also busy. I was getting so bored here so I thought I should grab a cup of chai from the tea stall parallel to my office. They gave the best chai.

I descended some of the stairs and Natasha was running upstairs.

"Where were you?" I asked. I probed her face and she had a mixed expression on her face.

"I...I..." She was stuttering a lot and I was getting bothered by her.

"Relax, come with me."

I took to her cabin and she sat on her olive green couch by the door.

I gave the glass of water resting on her main table. "Have it and calmly tell me what happened?"

She gulped the water slowly and her eyes were staring at me. She was making me scared.

She took a very deep breath and her mouth opened, "It is about Raghav." She stopped.

My heartbeat froze for a second and she continued, "Raghav met with an accident a week ago. Amit had given your contact to him as they both came back here. He was coming to meet you and...then a car hit him."

My heart froze once again. Blood felt cold and the brain stopped working. Those thoughts and feelings were right.

"Is he fine now? Where is he? I want to meet him." I was getting so panicked. My hands were shivering. My breaths were out of control. Sweat beads roll through the forehead.

"Relax, he is completely fine. It's been a week and...."

"And what Natasha? say it." I was still panicking and almost yelled at her.

"Raghav is waiting for you outside."

I stood up as I heard those calming words. My feet started to run as fast as they could and quickly descended the stairs so I could reach him as soon as possible. It seemed like these stairs were even taking so much time today.

I suddenly stopped because he was here in front of the office door. Wearing the black shirt he had worn when we first met. He was leaning on his car. My feet started to move toward him slowly and my face was glowing so much—I could feel it without looking in the mirror.

I wanted to hug him so badly but what was stopping me I had no idea. I wanted him to hug me and he listened to my inner voice because he expanded his arms and invited me for a warm, special, and so relaxing hug.

I quickly hugged him and when I lifted my head and looked into his eyes I asked him, "How are you now?"

"*Now*, I am fine." He never missed the chance to flirt with me.

But I stepped back and my face changed from a happy to an angry look. "You left without meeting me."

His smile went away and he said, "I need to take you somewhere."

"Where?" I asked him. I didn't like surprises. I was more of a curious person and right away I just wanted to know where he was going to take me.

"Let it be a surprise." He replied through his teeth.

I never wanted to disappoint him, not with any of my words or actions so, I didn't say the words: *I don't like surprises* but instead, I said, "Sure."

I was so elated to see him after weeks.

I texted Nat about this and she replied: **You have the right and perfect chance so don't waste it today. Love you.**

It was the evening time and the sun had dipped below the sky and left the hues of yellow and orange. My curiosity was getting higher and higher. But I was getting nervous as well.

He looked at me with a smile and then he looked to the road and he was repeating it for the third time now.

"What?" I asked with a laugh because he was looking so cute when he was doing that.

"You are looking so beautiful today."

"Is this compliment in exchange for revealing the name where we are going?"

He laughed softly because I guessed right and now he was pretending. "What no. I just don't want to ruin the surprise but I am saying sorry to you already because I am going to ruin your mood."

What is he going to say?

Now I was more nervous but I replied, "Okay."

We got out of the car and sat on the bench inside the Emerald Lake. I loved this place.

The view was so perfect to tell him what I felt for him but I wanted to listen to him first.

Is he also here to confess his feelings? This thought was making me more exhausted.

"Why are we here?" I asked with a delicate smile which could go any time.

"I want to be so clear with you." He cleared his throat.

"O..Okay."

"On the last day of our trip, I listened to words and..."

"and..." I repeated.

"Listen to me calmly, I know we both like each other and I am not angry at you, not at Karan. The thing is when someone goes very far away from you *then* you realize the importance of that person...and Karan is experiencing this with you."

He stopped for a second and I didn't disturb him. "Karan and you have been together for more than *twenty* years and this is a very long journey."

He sighed but continued, "I know I was your crush."

What does he know?

"Yes Aditi I knew but that can be just an

attraction because you were not happy with Karan and still, you are not happy with him and that's why you chose me because we met again."

I stopped him in between, "You are talking so wrong here, Raghav. This is not real you."

"I am just saying that you should give him a chance. Don't end this long journey because of *me*."

"Raghav you are not understanding. We don't feel for each other." My face was turning red. "I am not a toy. I was with him and I was not happy. I was with him because he supported me and took care of me after my parents but he started to behave so differently with me."

"But you loved him." He recalled.

"Like, I never *loved* him."

"That's why I said, he is seeing your value now. Give him a chance."

I didn't say anything for a few minutes.

"Do you love me?" I asked him.

He laughed. "I am not talking about myself. I am talking about you *two*. You don't even know me so well Aditi. But you have known him so well for many years."

"So you are saying that I should give him a chance and when everything goes well...I should continue with him and marry him?" My face was completely soaked in anger.

"NO, I...I mean yes." His voice seemed upset.

"Do you love me or not?"

"I do....okay.....I do but....on the last day in Coorg when you both were talking to each other. I heard you were saying to restart our relationship or something but I ignored it because Natasha told me that it was about friendship. I was in touch with her for the last week only."

He sighed, "Listen, He is not happy to see you going with someone else."

I didn't know what he was doing to me but I was done with him. If he wanted me to give Karan a chance then okay but I knew what was right for me.

"Okay, I accept what you say. I love you so much and I wanted to confess to you but our workshop was canceled and you left without telling me."

I cried, "Now I don't want to talk to you and I am leaving right now." I left from there and didn't turn back.

After coming back to the office I explained everything to Natasha and told her to keep quiet. I wanted to come home so she let me go.

I came home and again I didn't cry. Both of the boys had made me strong. I never thought that this Coorg trip was going to be not the best trip of mine but you didn't know about life when it digs a hole in front of you and you fall into its trap.

One wanted to come back into my life and the

one I truly love was sending me to *that person* I never experienced happiness with.

I would never understand. Why was Raghav so innocent after knowing everything about Karan?

At night, I cooked food for myself, played soft music on Spotify, and enjoyed the food alone. I didn't enjoy the food alone, I enjoyed my loneliness for the first time. After washing the dishes, I came to my room and I was ready to sleep. I was not allowing myself to cry or think unnecessary thoughts but I knew what to do now. It was my life and I was not going to give control of my life to any one of them.

Chapter 9

The days had passed—turned into weeks when I was fully committed to my work. I neither contacted Raghav nor Karan.

My work at Natasha's office was so hectic because I had to work on the computer for almost five to six hours with an hour lunch break but I was enjoying it after so many months. I didn't want to get stuck in that boring life because I always sought better options.

In these couple of months, a lot happened to me—my oldest best friend cum ex left me and then I met my old crush somehow again I met my ex on the same trip and again I left alone.

I needed time to process because all those things were simultaneously happening with me but one person was there with me all the time—Natasha. She offered me to stay with her in her house but I refused her offer because the more I stayed close to her, the more the distance grew, and when she was the one only left in my life, how could I let that disaster happen?

A WEEK LATER at lunchtime, Natasha and I decided to have lunch together in a restaurant that was ten minutes away from the office. I was packing some of my stuff when my phone's display popped up bright with a notification.

Karan....

Karan had texted me after months. The last time we talked was a few days after the Coorg trip.

"Hey, How are you, bestie?"

My eyes were wide open because I remembered he used to call me by this name when we were *dating* just to tease me in front of our friends and we were friends again. So why was he calling me that? I didn't want him to cross any lines and I hoped he didn't. But I had to be normal with him because he never forced me to come back to me as my *girlfriend.* I was angry at Raghav.

Only.

At.

Raghav.

"I am not your bestie anymore (Laugh emoji) and I am fine. How are you?"

(Heartbreak emoji) "I thought friends could be so casual but I messed everything up."

"Well, maybe but not in our case."

I typed quickly and my face had some creases on the forehead. I forgave him but I didn't want to talk to him every day.

"Are you coming or not?" Natasha asked.

"Coming....coming," I replied and put the phone inside my denim pocket.

The weather was so romantic today—a mild cold breeze, white fluffy cotton clouds on the blue canvas and the sun wanting to come out but clouds were not allowing him.

I let the gentle breeze play with my hair when I noticed Karan was standing in front of my office across the road with a bouquet.

I glared at Natasha and she made a face like. *God, why is he here now?* I could understand her situation because I also didn't want to meet him. I was not even expecting him here.

"I am waiting here. I am not going to cancel the plan." She said in a cranky tone because she booked the tables for us a long time ago.

"Okay, then come with me. I don't want to meet him alone "

"Okay." She agreed.

Natasha never refused me anything even if she didn't want to. She was a perfect example of a friend, not the one who was standing across the road.

We carefully crossed the road and he hugged

me casually like he did with everyone and then Natasha. He never hugged me in public and I was a little surprised.

He handed me the bouquet. "I know I am not allowed to disturb you this time but it is important."

"Okay, what's so important?" I asked.

He was behaving so unusually like something had changed in him. He was so quiet, and calm, and the most surprising thing was he was showing *love* by giving me the flowers.

"I know I have messed up everything and I am trying to be normal with you so if you remember tomorrow is my birthday and I want to celebrate it with you."

Natasha stared at me like she was saying *you can't go alone with him.*

But then Karan said again, "You're also invited, Nat."

I was happy for him if he wanted to change himself because at some point he needed to change himself. My heart wanted to give him a chance because he invited Nat and I was no one to ruin someone's birthday so, I agreed.

"Okay, we will come." I was not pretending to be so cool and normal with him because it came all naturally. If I showed him my happy hopeful face that *Oh my god, he is changing* then maybe he could understand it in another way.

"Okay, so be ready at 6 pm." Happiness was all over his face and after a long time he sat inside his car.

I felt happiness for him too. I was just praying that now he would not break my heart again.

"Are you serious?" Natasha turned toward me. "Why did you agree?"

"Look, I genuinely don't feel for him and now I have learned to move on, and after all, it's a bond of more than twenty years. I don't want to ruin his special day."

"I Don't think he's changed." Natasha was looking at him when he was many feet away from us.

At night when I was sitting at my desk with my laptop and posting some blogs, suddenly I thought of Karan. *How can I forget his birthday?*

His birthday was the day when we became friends for the first time in school. I was a partner in distributing candies to the teacher.

I thought again that I should go. But Natasha would also be there with me so there was no problem with that. But somewhere Natasha still didn't believe in Karan.

His birthday was tomorrow. I texted Natasha that if she was ready to go or not and immediately she replied and she had typed: **Well, how can I refuse this, if you are truly happy and going then** *there must be someone to protect you from that guy. (Wink emoji)*

Okay. I replied.

I should make his day special. After all, it is about birthdays.

Chapter 10

We reached his house and his friends were already there. Natasha didn't find it right at first because she saw Amit there and if he saw us he would ask us about our lives and of course Raghav which I didn't want to answer. *Or maybe he knew everything.*

After some time Karan showed up and we were constantly ignoring Amit. The music and the vibe were so catchy and perfect for Natasha to enjoy and she was in the mood to enjoy the party but she wasn't ready to leave me alone with him.

I was a bit bored and took out my phone but Karan was glaring at me. "Are you not enjoying the party?" He asked.

I immediately inserted the phone in my denim pocket and replied, "No...I was just checking the notification."

"Today is my day and you have to stop using your phone. Just enjoy the party."

The music changed to soft and slow and he offered his hand to dance with me. As I said I didn't want to spoil his day so I went on the floor with him. I was a little impressed because he maintained a good distance and after some time the music changed to a dancing number. Everyone started to enjoy it so much and I was also in the mood to dance with my heart out. *After so long.*

Those beautiful memories of *mine* were when we visited a special newly opened cafe where Karan and I celebrated his birthday because he wanted to cut the cake there.

When he was cutting his cake, those thoughts came to my mind. I was seriously glad to come to his birthday party today.

Natasha had just come out of the restroom and her happiness caught my attention. I got lost in her—She was married to a mature man who had no issue with her. He let her enjoy her life but sometimes I felt bad for her—she was so happy in her life with her loving husband but still couldn't have the happiness of children. I wanted her to be a mother someday and when she visited my home with her children I could play with them all the time.

AFTER CUTTING THE CAKE Karan came to me to drop me but he had a huge smile on his face today like he was up to something. Natasha had already gone with her husband but Karan didn't let me go for more minutes and somehow I managed to escape from Amit.

"I should go now, it's too late. Everyone is leaving." I said.

"Would you fulfill my last wish?" He asked me a favor.

"What?" I asked casually.

"Come with me."

He took me to a cafe where we celebrated *my* birthday for the first time after we started dating each other.

As I entered the cafe I didn't want to remember that memory I had with him but I was controlling too much. The cafe was so empty only two of us were there and some of the workers there.

"Why is this cafe empty and why are we here?"

"I know you want this on *your* birthday" He replied with a smile.

I was seriously so surprised because he still remembered that.

Oh god, why is he doing all this? Is he doing all this purposely? The thought made me suspicious of him.

We sat at the same table and had a plate of pasta with extra cheese resting there.

On my birthday I ordered pasta with extra cheese and he still remembered it.

Something is not going well here.

"I ordered one more thing that you may have

forgotten. Here it is." Karan pointed excitedly to the waiter who was bringing two plates of golden French fries with fried fish, and cheesecake.

How can I forget about this?

"You still remember?" I asked while a small smile on my face stuck.

"How can I Aditi, it was your first dinner date with me here."

"hmm."

He didn't need to say unnecessary things.

After we were done with the food. The main chef brought the cake and it was the same cake *I* cut on my birthday. My hands were shaking now because it was getting too much. I looked at him and he was smiling—He was smiling like he had won a battle.

What is he trying to do?

He cut the cake and the staff wished him, singing the birthday song and I didn't want to even clap. I was just faking my happiness now. In his home, I was genuinely elated for him but what's he doing now was not necessary.

Once again, the feeling of weirdness came back.

I think Natasha was right about him.

He extended his hand toward me with a smile. I didn't let him feed me. I took the cake piece gently and inserted it in his mouth. He was unhappy with this but now I didn't care.

We came out of the cafe and I was not feeling well because of his recent actions but I was missing Raghav. Now I was regretting fulfilling his last wish. Nothing seemed well now but somehow I spent the whole day.

He had cut two cakes because I also cut two cakes back then and I didn't know why he wanted me to recall every memory with him—I didn't want to. It was midnight and we were heading home.

Outside my apartment, he stood and waited to say something, "Thank you so much for today."

I nodded with an uncomfortable smile.

"I wanted to meet you tomorrow." He said.

"But I have an office."

"Please, meet me at my home. At 7 pm. Ok bye." He said and he just walked away.

What's so wrong with him today?

NEXT EVENING, I didn't want to go to his house. After office, I went directly home. I had decided to make some excuses.

When I came out of the bathroom after taking a shower. Someone knocked on the door and I had a feeling that Karan was behind the door. I opened and he was there in front of me. Now I didn't have any chance to make any excuses.

"Sorry to disturb but can you come with me?" He asked nervously.

"It's not possible, Karan. I have just come home

and where do you want to go this time?" I asked.

"Please come. I want to confess something."

I could not argue with him because I was tired of all such things.

"Okay fine." I threw the comb on the bed and followed him.

When we reached his house. He was jiggling a key in his hand with a smile.

"What are you doing?" I asked with a cranky expression.

"Trying to find the right key."

Wow, he doesn't know his house key.

He inserted the key and yanked open the door.

"Can you close your eyes?" He requested.

"What? Why?" Weird sensations spread all over my body.

"Please."

"Fine."

We both entered and carefully helped me when I opened my eyes my mind was about to explode.

The room was fully covered with roses on the floor with some red *heart-shaped* balloons and fairy lights on the corner of the room. I didn't want to waste my time so I shook my head and asked. "What is that?" I turned around and he was already on his knees, both of his hands holding a box of a ring that was open. A minimal metal ring rests inside the box.

Is he mad? Why is he proposing to me?

"What are you doing, Karan?"

"Shhh, Just listen to me."

"No, don't do this to me. Stand up or I am leaving."

I was not ready to fall for him again.

"Wait Aditi, let me say it." He took a deep breath and said, "Will you marry me, Aditi?"

"Why are you doing this to me, Karan? We are done. You wanted to remain friends."

He didn't stand up and said, "I know I was a foolish guy. But now I want you back in my life."

"Why are you doing all this drama here?" I was getting so pissed off.

"This is not a drama, Aditi. I genuinely feel for you."

"But I do not and I never loved you."

I started to leave the room but he quickly came in front of me and closed the door. "Why are you doing this? Why can't you come back to me? We have been together since childhood and how can you forget everything in just a month?"

I wanted to punch him in the face *again* but I controlled myself again because this was high time to talk to him. I took a deep breath.

"Because I love Raghav not you. Since the time we were in college. I had a *huge crush* on him but something happened and I accepted your proposal.

The biggest mistake of my life. During these years I was happy with you when we were only best friends but you as a boyfriend—a terrible person. And the last thing, Raghav and I are dating—we are in a relationship." I lied, why? I didn't know.

"What?" He was frozen in his place like he had seen some ghost behind me or in me. "You are dating him?"

"So you are not shocked that I was in love with him in our college days but you are more concerned if I am dating him now?"

He stood up and threw the box of the ring so hard and his face turned red. This was the Karan that I never liked and that's why I hated his impulsive nature.

"Well, I already knew you liked him. That's why I proposed to you as soon as I could because I knew as we were friends for years you would only accept me. How can I let you be for someone else? You are only mine okay." Those words were hurting me more than when I was with him in a horrible cage.

I was so shocked because he knew. He never met Raghav or saw him in college. Still, he knew and that's why he proposed to me.

He never loved me. He just can't see me with anyone else.

"So, you never loved me and you were the one who wanted to end this and now I don't want to get back to you. We are done, Karan. I don't love you. I only love Raghav and now don't you dare to touch me ever again."

Karan calmed himself and laughed but his eyes were wet. "Raghav changed you. He made you a rebellion."

"No, Karan, *you* changed me. I was a scared cat with you." I opened the door and left. I came back to my home and I didn't cry but I smiled and I was so proud of myself. There was a time when I couldn't live without Karan but today he taught me how to stay without him.

I saw myself in the mirror and said to my reflection: *I am so proud of you Aditi.*

Chapter 11

I didn't tell Natasha what Karan did to me last night.

He still didn't love me. He just couldn't see me with anybody. He wanted to control my life and I could not let that happen. But this morning a thought came to my mind when he was glaring at me with the ring. It seemed he was telling his true feelings because he always used to hate talking about marriage and I had to calm him down by saying this: *I am sorry, I am not going to talk about our marriage until and unless you are ready.*

I still remember I used to cry in front of him all the time and he just stared at me like he would beat me although he never raised his hand at me—but he still had a bad temper.

He broke up the relationship and I didn't even ask the reason and again he wanted me back in his life. Ragav was right about him but Raghav was not right when he was forcing me to go and settle with him.

Today I was missing Raghav so much. We

haven't talked for many days. Although he tried to contact Nat.

I was remembering his innocence. I knew he loved me but still, he wanted to give us a chance so that we could get back together.

But I was so fed up with those mixed feelings towards Raghav and Karan. I didn't want to get tangled in them. I wanted to live my life as I wanted. I loved Raghav but he didn't want to stay with me and what Karan did to me was so strange. I had never imagined that Karan would make me feel alone. I was so baffled once again.

I was on my desk clicking my pen on the table and not feeling so good. My face was so pale and Natasha was even telling me that I did not look as happy as I was before Karan's birthday.

Sometimes I thought because of me she deprived herself of happiness because she was a happy soul like a child and even if I pretended that I was happy too, she caught me that I was acting.

She came to me and informed me, "Aditi, you have to go to Bangalore. There is a new restaurant that has opened and I have already sent your name there and they have approved because they have seen your Instagram page and they believe you can cover them so perfectly."

But I had decided something else and I had to tell her soon. I wanted to answer her but her phone rang and she was behaving a little awkwardly. She was behaving like she wanted to answer that phone but not in front of me.

"Excuse me." Her face was a little pale.

She sat on the corner and almost whispered and tried to glare at me if I was not listening to her. I was not interested in eavesdropping.

She finished her talk and came back to me. I didn't notice that I had tears in my eyes. I was getting so baffled about whether I should consider Karan's feelings, talk to Raghav about my feelings, or avoid everything and focus on my traveling work.

Natasha sat next to me and asked, "Hey, why are you crying?"

She put her phone on the table. I wanted to say *nothing* but my mouth said, "I am missing Raghav."

She hugged me and I let myself cry and she didn't even stop me.

She loosened her grip on me and commented, "I am sure these tears are not only because you are missing him. Something has happened to you."

I wiped my tears and I sobbed so badly.

"Tell me what happened?" She asked.

I took a deep breath and threw out from my heart what pissed me off last night because of Karan.

"Karan came to my house last night and he

took me to his house. He wanted to talk about something important. Firstly I was not ready to go with him but then he insisted so I went." I stopped and took a deep breath again.

"It's okay, just say it." She rubbed my arm gently.

"His house was decorated *romantically*."

Natasha stared at me with shock.

I nodded and continued, "I was so angry at first when I saw the decoration and then he kneeled and... and... he... he proposed to me for.... marriage."

Natasha was also stunned and she was not saying anything because I knew there was nothing to say but she asked, "Do you feel for Karan?"

I paused for a second and didn't reply to her.

"Aditi." Natasha was saying my name. "I know it could be hard for you but if you don't feel for him then stop thinking about him."

"I am tired of both of them. I want to live a life where I can be genuinely happy in my life even if I am alone." I cried.

"I can understand, tell me what you are thinking?" She hugged me. "If you are thinking that...then please don't think that. I request you."

Somewhere she knew that I wanted a separate life.

"I am sorry Nat, I have to do this." I picked up my bag and left for my home.

Chapter 12
six months later...

"How can I help you?" I asked the customer oh sorry, *a reader.* I was not allowed to say customers because in this bookstore whoever was coming and buying books were our *lovely readers* not only a buyer.

"I want to talk to you. Can you come with me to the romance section? I can't find the right book." The lady asked for help.

"Of course, after you," I said politely.

I followed her, and when we reached the romance section, she looked left and right, and no one was there. She hugged me too tightly. I also didn't leave her, and she was not letting me go. Then finally after a minute, she stepped away.

"It has been three weeks this time and you haven't met me, why?" Natasha asked with teary eyes.

I replied, "I am sorry but I missed you so much, Nat, and please don't cry." I also controlled myself to not cry in front of her. "I am living with my grandparents after almost *five* years and they are also glad to have me back. That's why I got so busy."

She nodded. "I am sorry but I am happy for you that you have started a fresh life as you wanted and now you are living with *your* family—you always wanted a family."

"Yeah, I am more *proud* than *happy* because I chose no one but my family but still if Raghav is not going to be with me then no one takes his place." I smiled when I said his name.

"Are you sure, my girl?" A soft familiar voice came from the other side of the shelf. I turned around and gorgeous chocolate brown eyes were glaring at me through the gaps between shelf planks.

It's him—It's Raghav.

The tears were rolling down. I wanted to hug him so badly. I walked toward him by crossing the shelf and stood in front of him. A smile appeared on my face but my feet stopped and then the smile slowly faded away. His words started to dance in my head: *You should give him a second chance.* I backed off from there.

I left the bookstore and controlled myself but as Natasha followed me and put her hand on my shoulder I burst out in tears. She hugged me and said those words which I hated the most, "Give him a chance. He has something important to say."

I backed my steps and sharply asked with a sob, "Why is he here? He didn't want to spend his life with me. He wanted me to stay with that guy who was so wrong for me and he was telling me to go to him and give him a second chance? Now you want me to give *Raghav* a chance? Is my life a joke?"

I knew Nat was on my side. I was just so baffled because, after six months of happy life, my life again became abnormal.

My hand felt a jerk and my body too. Raghav

pulled me toward him and said gently, "You have to listen to me okay? Now I am asking for a chance. Please, Aditi." He was grabbing my arm not so hard but gently because he could never hurt me—it was so obvious in his eyes. The way he pulled me closer—The old feeling of being safe around him came again.

Those feelings of only listening to him came back again.

"At least listen to him—it is about Karan and it is so important," Natasha insisted.

I took a pause and let the fresh breeze come to me. After thinking for a few minutes I agreed to talk to him. I wiped my eyes. "Okay, come with me." I took him to the rooftop of the bookstore. This was the most calm place here. Whenever I was not feeling good-I came here.

"Wow, this is so peaceful." He complimented.

"Sit." I ignored him.

But yes, it was so peaceful because I decorated this rooftop and made one corner into a reading nook.

He sat on the chair. He was observing here and there. He looked at my books.

"You started reading too."

"What do you want to talk about?" I asked.

He sighed and smiled like always. His smile was one of my favorites and I had seen this smile after more than half a year.

"Firstly, I missed you so much."

"But you wanted it for a lifetime," I replied in a rude tone.

He chuckled. "Well, now I am so guilty of what I said to you."

"Because I am far away and you might have understood the importance of a person?" I replied sarcastically.

"No, Aditi. I am serious. I was just giving you both a chance. I wanted to save a relationship but I was so stupid." His forehead had tensed lines. "I am sorry, I was sending you to the person who was not meant for you."

"Our relationship ended because *he* doesn't want to continue with me. *You* were nowhere then." I said sharply. "And I was trying to tell you that *Karan* was not for me but *you* are."

"That's why I am here." He held my both hands and once again I let him do what he was doing. "I am so sorry for what I did to you. I was so stupid then. Now I know everything about Karan and I am here so that you can end this relationship with him NOW because..." He took a deep sigh.

"Because what?" I could feel something was not good.

I could feel he was worried.

He said, "Because his father....his father....."

"His father what, Raghav?" I was so tense because he was sweating and he was stuttering a lot.

"I am sorry but his father...killed your parents."

My body was freezing like someone had hit a hammer on my head. I couldn't feel anything around me. I was overwhelmed by a storm of emotion.

I could see Raghav was shaking me but his voice had frozen and not reached my ears. Only his lips were moving. I felt an intense sense of betrayal, anger, and shock.

A constant thought was running in my mind: *How could People I trusted so deeply have done something so horrific?*

The pain of losing my parents came rushing back, but now it's mixed with this unbearable truth.

When I tried to say something I asked him, "Does Karan know about this?" I was praying that he must not be aware of that.

"Yes, he knows and that's why he wanted to break up with you. He didn't want to live with you with a horrible secret and how can he ask his father about this? But don't worry, his father is behind bars as soon as I got everything Amit and I sent him where he must belong."

I was torn apart inside. I liked Karan once and trusted him blindly because he supported me too much, and took care of me too much. But I didn't know he was a good person but because of his father he used to stay uncomfortable with me. It must be so hard for him in these years.

"But you know who supported me in this?"

I shook my head.

"Karan."

"Karan?" My heart sank.

"Yes, he was in so much guilt in these years. He was only trying to save his father because he's father and he doesn't want to lose you either but he couldn't tell you."

"Why did his father do this to them?"

"A few days ago Karan came to my home. He was so anxious and he told me that he wanted to say something. Firstly he told me that he understood about us and he told me....you loved *me*." He smiled and continued. "He said to me that he always loved you but because of this darkest secret of his life he couldn't move further with you. How could he be happy when he knows his father killed *your parents*."

I was crying but after a few seconds I managed to ask, "Why did his father kill them?"

"Your parents and his father started a business together but it failed because of *your...father*. Your father almost stole everything from him. I am so sorry to tell you this, Aditi but you have the right to know about your parents. That's why you are still living with your *Nana and Nani*. Your father was not a good man—he used to be a criminal and your mother also supported him and one day when Karan's father got the chance he killed both of them."

The feeling and the clear memories of both of them came in front of my eyes. *That's why Mummy and Papa got rich suddenly.*

"And one more thing, when Karan was telling me all these things—the police were waiting for him outside. He surrendered himself but trust me, There was so much guilt in his eyes."

I cried so badly. My hands were shivering. I didn't know who to trust now.

"You are accusing my parents, Raghav."

"I knew about it because it is uneasy to believe about your parents. I know it is too horrific but..." He took out some papers and showed the truth. The papers were showing me they both stole their property and factory.

The confusion and hurtness were almost too much to bear. It was utterly devastated.

"I can understand, everyone you loved betrayed you and I am sorry. I also left you in this horrible situation but you needed to know the truth. Don't be harsh on yourself Aditi." He pressed my head to his chest and let me cry until I calmed down.

I released my head from his hands and wiped all my tears. I was so calm now. I was so strong now and one thought was revolving around my mind: Why was I crying and for whom? For those who betrayed me, who hid their true identities all the time? Now I wanted to forget everything.

My past was so terrible but now I didn't want to make my present and future that way. I hugged Raghav once again and said, "I want to forget everything whatever happened. I want to make my life the best with you. I love you so much, Raghav."

I stood up and searched for my paper ring. I used to make paper rings whenever I missed Raghav. But today I made a ring with daisy flowers and sat in front of him and asked, "Will you marry me, my photographer?"

He came closer with a broad smile and lifted me in his arms. "How can I say no, *my girl.*"

We both were smiling so broadly. He put me down and our lips pressed together.

Everything happens for a reason.

Chapter 13

Two months later....

"Are you ready, my girl?" He asked while sitting in the driving seat.

I checked my seatbelt and he was still glaring at me.

"What?" I asked while playing a song in the car.

"How can I drive? You distract me a lot." He gave me a peck on my cheek. I didn't know where we were going.

I turned my head a bit to the back of the car and there was a picnic basket on the backseat. I didn't say anything because I didn't want to ruin his surprise but now I could tell that we were going to a PICNIC DATE.

"Our first meeting was also a road trip and today after a year it is still a road trip." I got curious.

"Yes." He started the car. "Tell me, why do you love to travel so much? You always get so curious."

I gave him a fleeting smile and replied, "I love to travel because it's not just the place, it's about unraveling the story of existence itself." I paused and smiled, "And our destiny wanted us to meet again, since then I can't live without traveling."

"I think the same." He winked.

I looked outside from the window and Emerald Lake was here. This was one of the most beautiful places in Ooty and it was my favorite. I remembered last time when we came here it was such a horrible experience for me but suddenly I also remembered Karan.

Karan never went to jail. Raghav didn't let him go. He loved me a lot but he was happy after seeing Raghav and me together and I also wanted to forget everything because I was not going back to him and I could not change the past.

I wanted to start fresh and Raghav and I were planning to marry next month.

"So are you ready for the picnic date with me?" He confessed.

"What? We are here for a picnic?" I pretend to fake my surprised actions.

We got out of the car. After reaching beside the lake, he took out a white sheet and two cushions. He came towards me and said, "You are a terrible actor."

Seriously? Was I that bad?

"Are you helping me or not?" He asked.

I quickly followed him and we spread the white sheet on the soft grass by the lake. The view here was so surreal, surrounded by lush greenery and rolling hills. The lake was so calm and still. The reflection of clouds added depth to the view.

It was a perfect place for nature lovers.

By the time I admired all the beauty we were surrounded by, Raghav had made all the arrangements.

I didn't see the beauty before but today I was admiring every inch of the surroundings.

There were chocolate muffins, soft drinks, a flower boutique with some romance books on it, a box of pizza, some fresh berries, a bottle of water, and a tablet—maybe for a movie. Everything was so perfect here.

He offered me his hand and I hopped on the sheet carefully so I didn't mess everything up. We both sat in our place so close to each other but I must say the sheet he had brought was small. So we didn't have any other option and we had to sit close to each other.

The air was cool and a light breeze was playing with our hair gently. Our eyes reflected the colors of the sky—pink and warm orange.

"This is so perfect. I wish I could do this for you."

"It is the same thing, don't worry."

I sensed a very attached and close sense of belonging as he finished the sentence. We were dating each other but we never proposed officially yet.

With a soft chuckle, we started our picnic and

he played a comedy movie on the table instead of a romantic one. Raghav was so different from others and that's why I fell for him so quickly in Coorg because in our college time, I didn't know about him.

During this whole picnic, we both were laughing and enjoying ourselves and we were just living the moment together.

After some time the darkness took place in the whole sky and stars were popping up on the grayish black sky. Our picnic was also done. This picnic was so delightful.

"Thank you so much for this. It is one of the most beautiful days I have lived in my life." I showed my gratitude to him because it was seriously so perfect.

"This is not all, Aditi." He came closer and held my both hands. "I wanted to tell you something for ages."

He closed his eyes. There was silence for a few seconds and he opened his eyes and confessed, "Aditi, I love you. I love you so much. From the moment I saw you for the first time—my life has been filled with joy and purpose. I didn't used to believe in love but as I saw you, and observed you—I immediately started to like you. I never wanted to come to college but after seeing you in your floral pastel yellow dress I fell for you and since then I never missed any of my art classes."

"Are you..."

"Yes Aditi, I have liked you since college days. I was crazy about you. I was coming to propose to you."

"Then why did you not?" I asked.

"I got nervous and scared of the thought of what if you reject me but after that day I tried again but it was so late. Karan had already proposed to you."

My eyes were so wet—I was crying from inside. In these years, I had to spend my life with a person who I never loved.

"Why are you crying, Aditi? Did I hurt you?" He asked so innocently.

Without thinking twice I hugged him. I let him wrap his hand around myself and I let myself sink in at that moment. I cried so hard on his chest and he kept asking me.

He lost his grip firmly and I confessed to him, "I had lost my parents when I was eighteen. I was in school and I started to live with my maternal grandparents. Karan became my best friend in school and he was my only best friend. This friendship continued till the third year. When my parents died I needed support and Karan was the person. but it is not about him—it is about you."

I stopped myself, let myself take some breaths and continued, "Then I saw you in the third year and almost half of the girls in our college were behind you. I had a crush on you instantly when I heard about you. I know you are my senior but I want to stop myself from following you wherever you go."

"And *you* followed me in the library, not your friend." He quickly spoke up like he would miss the chance.

I nodded shyly.

"But when I got to know that you are going to marry and I saw your post after two months on Instagram, I was broken and I finally said yes to Karan."

He laughed and laughed and laughed. "I had to marry an unknown girl because I saw Karan proposing to you and my parents were also forcing me to marry because I am too old." He laughed again.

I also laughed but I laughed at our fates. "How our destiny has played a trick on us, we both liked each other for so many years but due to some misunderstanding we had to spend our time with the wrong people."

He hugged me again, "Now we are together forever. I am not going to leave you now. I have waited for more than four years, two months, and twenty-eight days Aditi, So, will you marry me?" He asked the right question at the right time.

"Of course I will. After all, I have also waited for four years, two months, and twenty-eight days."

We both chuckled softly. "I also love you, my photographer." I said.

We stepped back from the hug and he kissed me on my forehead. Our forehead rests together with a smile.

One thought was making me crazy because I had no idea that I was his crush too.

We laid down on the sheet after putting the stuff back in the basket and stargazing together—hand in hand. We captured ourselves in his camera which he took out at the end of the picnic and this was a memory to cherish forever.

He looked into my eyes and said, "Will you go with me?"

"Where?" I asked curiously.

"on a road trip." He *smiled.*

THE END!!

And they lived happily ever after...

<u>Upcoming novel in 2025</u>

#Ink stains and coffee beans

ABOUT AUTHOR

She has been pursuing her dream since she wrote her first poetry three years ago. She started with poetry and ended up writing *Romance stories*. She will write fantasy novels as well because she wrote and published her first book of the fantasy genre in 2021 and it was a huge fail. Since then she's been working so hard.

For more details

Contact her on her Instagram handle:
@talesbyritika